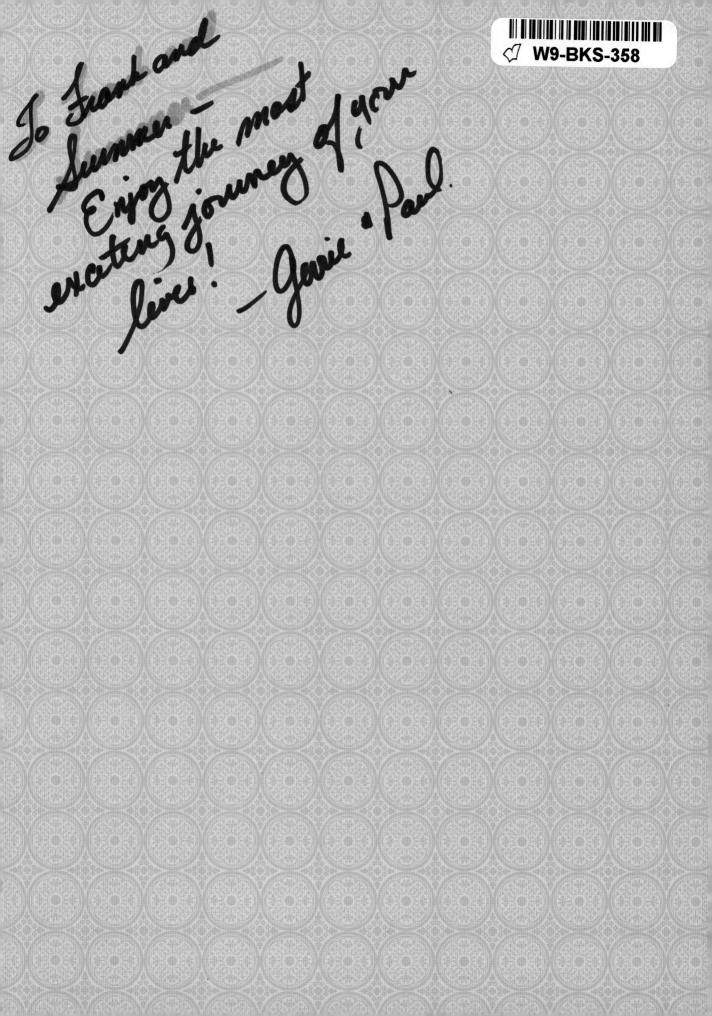

To Frank and
Summer —
Enjoy the most
exciting journey of you
lives!
— Janie & Paul.

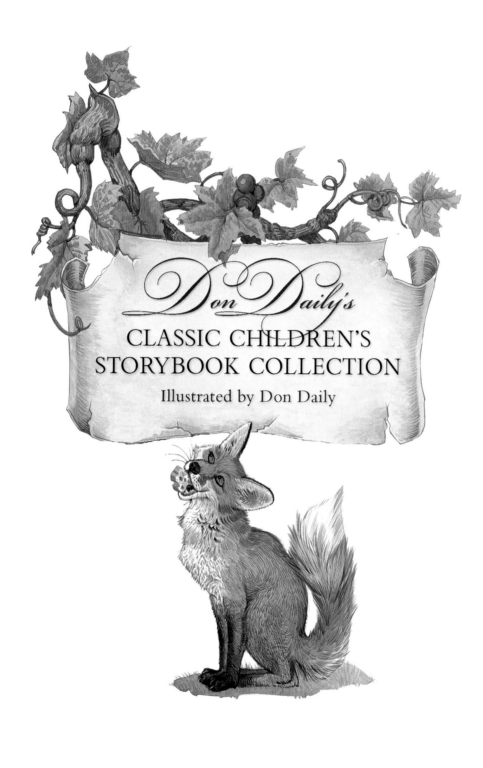

Don Daily's
CLASSIC CHILDREN'S
STORYBOOK COLLECTION

Illustrated by Don Daily

COURAGE
BOOKS

AN IMPRINT OF RUNNING PRESS
PHILADELPHIA • LONDON

9 8 7 6 5 4 3 2 1
Digit on the right indicates the number of this printing

Library of Congress Control Number: 2006923158
ISBN-13: 978-0-7624-2727-7
ISBN-10: 0-7624-2727-2

Designed by Frances J. Soo Ping Chow
Edited by Elizabeth Encarnacion
Typography: Bembo and Fruitger

This book may be ordered by mail from the publisher.
But try your bookstore first!

Published by Courage Books, an imprint of
Running Press Book Publishers
125 South Twenty-Second Street
Philadelphia, Pennsylvania 19103-4399

Visit us on the web!
www.runningpress.com

Portions of this work have previously appeared
in other books by Running Press Book Publishers

TABLE OF CONTENTS

DON DAILY (1940-2002) was an alumnus of the Art Center College of Design in Los Angeles. He was also an honored member of the Society of Illustrators, as well as a certified member of the American Portrait Society.

Don Daily has illustrated *The Classic Tales of Brer Rabbit*, *The Classic Treasury of Aesop's Fables*, *The Classic Treasury of Grimm's Fairy Tales*, *The Jungle Book*, and *The Wind in the Willows*, among others. His whimsical illustrations of children's classics continue to delight readers of all ages.

Old Mother Goose, when
She wanted to wander,
Would ride through the air
On a very fine gander.

Humpty Dumpty sat on a wall,
Humpty Dumpty had a great fall;
All the king's horses, and all the king's men
Couldn't put Humpty Dumpty together again.

Peter, Peter, pumpkin-eater,

Had a wife and couldn't keep her;

He put her in a pumpkin shell,

And there he kept her very well.

Hansel and Gretel

There was once a young boy and girl that lived at the edge of a great, dark forest with their loving father, a woodcutter, and evil stepmother, who never cared very much for the children. A great famine had come over the land and there was barely a thing to eat.

With little food to go around, times were hard and the woodcutter's wife placed the blame on the children. The woman knew that if the children were no longer their concern, then she and her husband would have plenty to eat between them. She cooked up an evil plan to get rid of little Hansel and Gretel, once and for all.

Late one night, when the children were fast asleep in their beds, the woodcutter spoke of the troubles his family faced.

"I have thought and thought, and searched as much as any man could. There is no food to feed our little ones, not to mention ourselves," the woodcutter said, his brow furrowed with worry.

"Do not fret, my love. I have already come up with the perfect solution. The forest is rich with fruits and berries. We can leave the children there to live. There is no other way for all of us to survive."

"I only hope that you are right," the woodcutter said reluctantly.

"You needn't worry, my dear. I've thought it through well."

What the sinister woman had not realized was that the children had been nearby listening the whole time.

"Oh Gretel, what ever will we do?"

"Perhaps we could sneak back to the house once our stepmother has left. But how will we ever find our way back home?" Gretel asked with a worried tone.

The next afternoon, as Hansel and Gretel finished up their chores, their stepmother gathered them together for an outing in the forest to gather fruits and berries. They were each given a dry piece of bread to eat for their supper.

As the two children walked along through the forest, Hansel realized that he could break the bread into crumbs and leave a trail to lead them back home.

They gathered berries and grew quite tired with the work of the day. Their stepmother assured them that she would finish the work as they rested there for a little while. When Hansel and Gretel had settled into a deep sleep, their stepmother ran off, leaving them alone in the darkness of the forest.

Hansel and Gretel awoke to find themselves surrounded by the eerie sounds of night, and the moon shining brightly above them.

"Gretel! Let's go. We will just follow the trail of crumbs."

But when the children began to look for the trail that Hansel had left, there was nothing to be found. The little creatures of the forest had eaten up all of the bread-crumbs. They were left with no way to get home.

Hansel and Gretel searched everywhere for the path, but it was no use. Each direction they turned looked the same as the last. After spend-ing most of the night hopelessly wandering about, they snuggled together against the trunk of a grand tree.

As morning stretched over the forest, they awoke to the sound of a bird singing. They followed the song of the little bird, and it led them to the most magnificent house either of them had ever seen.

It was a little cottage, but unlike the cottages that they knew. It was made of gingerbread and icing, its windows of the purest sugar, and its roof consisted of cake and gumdrops.

"Food, Hansel! We've found food!" cried Gretel with much glee, as she broke a piece of the roof from its place and began to eat. Hansel, sharing in his sister's excitement, began to taste one of the windows.

From within the gingerbread walls came a quiet voice: *Nibbling, nibbling like a mouse. Who's that nibbling at my house?*

The children were giddy with their discovery, and to the chant they replied: *We will not lie. We'll tell the truth. It's the wind that nibbles at your roof.*

The children thought little of the voice and continued to feed on the sugary goodness of the house. Suddenly, the door of the cottage swung open and out stepped an ugly, old woman.

"Hello my children. Why are you here eating my humble little home?" asked the old woman.

"Please don't be angry," begged the children. "Our evil stepmother left us here in the forest to die. We've had nothing to eat and we're so very hungry. Please forgive us for eating your cottage."

The woman looked at the children with a toothless smile and said, "You children should join me inside for a bite to eat." Once they were inside, the children enjoyed all the milk and pancakes their bellies could hold. Once they were full, the old woman tucked them snugly into bed.

But as the children slept, the kind old woman who had helped them seemed to change. Her face grew mean and cold. For she wasn't a kind old woman at all, but rather an evil witch. And the evil witch loved nothing more than eating little children.

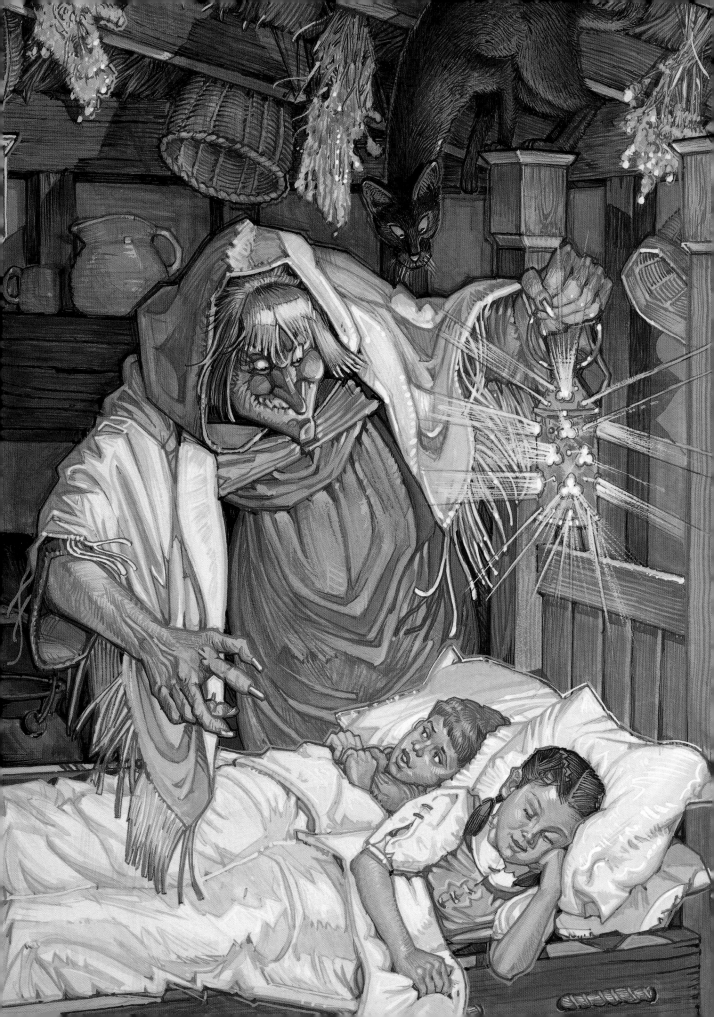

There she sat, watching her meal. I think that I will eat the boy first, as the girl will take much more work.

She quietly scooped Hansel up from his warm comfortable spot, and locked him in a large cage that she kept hidden. Hansel screamed and yelled for Gretel to help him, but when Gretel awoke, Hansel was already behind the bars of the great cage.

"Yes, yes, get up, little one," said the evil witch to Gretel, "It is almost time that I feast on your brother. But first you shall fatten him up for me. Now, cook him something filling to eat!"

Without Hansel to help her, there was little that Gretel could do. And so, she obeyed the witch's commands, and spent the day feeding Hansel all that he could eat.

The witch would check, every so often, to see if Hansel was quite ready. "Give me your finger," the witch would say. But instead of his finger, Hansel would stick out a small twig that he had found at the bottom of the cage.

"Not any fatter! Not the tiniest bit fatter!" cried the witch. "Girl, you must make him more food! He is still far too thin to eat."

After many days had passed, the witch gave up on trying to fatten up the boy.

"It has been long enough! I can wait no longer. It is time for your brother to be cooked." She instructed Gretel to check the temperature of the oven—
it had to be hot enough.

Gretel looked over at the large oven and realized that the witch
had yet another plan. As soon as Gretel crawled into the
oven, the witch would push her in and slam the door shut.
But Gretel was too smart to fall for the witch's trick.

"I do not know how to check the oven, ma'am."

"What do
you mean, child?

Simply crawl inside and check that the

oven is quite hot enough!"

"I don't think that I will fit," said Gretel to the witch.

"Of course you will fit," yelled the witch as she undid her apron and stuck her

head into the oven. Gretel wasted no time and ran right up behind the witch and

gave a great PUSH! She quickly closed the oven door and locked it with a wooden

spoon, slipped right through the handles.

"Let me out of here! Let me out!" cried the witch. "I promise to never eat any

child ever again!"

But Gretel paid no attention to the witch's cries and went at once to release her

brother. Once Hansel was free, the two children ran outside, happy to be away from

that wicked witch.

But they still were unsure of which way to go. They heard the familiar song of a little bird, and when

they looked up, they found

the same bird that had led them to the cottage.

"Thank you, dear children. You have at last released me from the witch's evil spell,

and I can once again fly free," said the bird. "Is there any way that I can repay you?"

"Can you take us home?" asked Gretel.

"Just follow me, and I will have you back home in no time at all."

When they reached their cottage, they found their

father chopping wood, but there was no sign of

their awful stepmother.

"Father, we're home!" cried the children.

"Oh, my dears! How happy I am to see

you," exclaimed their father. "I have not slept a wink

since you have been gone. I've missed you so much!"

He then told of how their stepmother

had died during their time in the

forest, and how he had been so all alone.

"But now, with my little Hansel and Gretel

back home, life is good once again!"

And they all lived happily ever after.

The Lion and the Mouse

A mouse was wandering through the jungle, not paying any attention to where he was going. Suddenly he realized that he had climbed onto the back of a huge, sleeping lion.

"Uh-oh," the mouse thought as he tried to slowly tiptoe off. The lion, tickled by the mouse's feet, reached up to scratch. When he felt the mouse, he awakened.

"What's this?" roared the lion as he grabbed the trembling creature.

Slowly he lifted the mouse to his mouth. The poor mouse could see the lion's sharp teeth and feel his hot breath as he was pulled closer and closer.

"Please sir," squeaked the mouse. "I . . . I didn't mean to disturb your sleep. Please don't harm me. If you spare my life, one day I'll save yours."

"Ha ha," laughed the mighty lion. "How can you help me? You amuse me, little mouse, and because you do, I'll let you go."

The mouse scurried off as soon as his feet reached the ground.

Many months went by, and the mouse kept as far away from the lion as possible. Then one day he heard the most pitiful moaning. He followed the sound, which led him to the lion, who was hopelessly tangled in a hunter's trap.

"Mr. Lion, sir" said the mouse, "a while ago I promised to repay your kindness. Today, I shall keep my word."

Right away, the mouse went to work gnawing at the ropes that held the lion. In no time, the lion was free.

"Mouse," said the lion, "I did not believe that the likes of you could ever rescue me, but now I know you are a true friend."

LITTLE FRIENDS MAY BECOME GREAT FRIENDS.

Brer Fox, Brer Rabbit, Brer Bear, and the Peanut Patch

rer Fox had the best peanut patch in the country. It was full of lush, green vines bursting with plump peanuts that were just about to ripen. All the other creatures on the Old Plantation were mighty envious of Brer Fox—except for Brer Rabbit.

Brer Rabbit would

have been envious, too, if he hadn't found a

way to take advantage of the situation. Brer Rabbit decided to

wait until the peanuts were ripe, and then sneak through a hole in the fence to

snatch whatever peanuts he could.

Sure enough, just as soon as the peanuts were ripe, Brer Fox got up bright and

early to check on his patch. Right away he discovered that someone had been steal-

ing peanuts right off the vine!

Brer Fox was furious at the robber for ruining all his hard work, and he was determined to catch the thief. Walking

around the outskirts of the patch, he found a hole in the

fence—a hole just the right size for a crafty rabbit to slip through. Right there, Brer

Fox set a trap. He bent down the branch of an old hickory tree that stood beside the

fence, and tied a rope to the end of it. At the other end of the rope he tied a loop,

and he set that loop down in front of the hole in the fence, and weighed it down

with a rock. Then he covered it with leaves and grass.

Whoever stepped into that trap would be caught in the loop

and strung up in the hickory tree by the leg. Brer Fox was pleased

with himself. Now he could catch the thief. That night, when

Brer Rabbit sneaked through the hole for more peanuts, he

stepped right into the trap. When he kicked away the rock, the

loop flew up around his leg, dragging him up into the air between

heaven and earth. He was mighty surprised to find himself

swinging upside-down from the hickory tree.

I hope I don't fall, thought Brer Rabbit, swinging back and

forth. Then he had another thought: I hope I do fall—other-

wise, I might not get down. And there he hung, swinging

back and forth and thinking, trying to fig-

ure out what to tell Brer Fox to get

out of this one.

Just as the sun began to rise,

Brer Rabbit heard someone lumbering up the road behind him. By and by, Brer Bear ambled on up to the tree and saw Brer Rabbit hanging there, upside-down.

"Howdy, Brer Rabbit," said Brer Bear, tilting his head to look Brer Rabbit in the face. "How are you doing this fine morning?"

Brer Rabbit smiled a big smile. "Very fine, Brer Bear, very fine. No sir, you won't catch me complaining today!"

Brer Bear was puzzled—but it wasn't hard to puzzle Brer Bear.

"What are you doing hanging up there in the elements, Brer Rabbit?" he asked.

"Well, truth be told, Brer Bear, I'm making a dollar a minute," said Brer Rabbit.

"A dollar a minute! How?"

"Brer Fox is paying me to keep watch over his peanut patch," Brer Rabbit explained. "Some thief has been stealing his goobers. Yessir, this is just about the best job I've ever had. Hanging upside-down gives you a whole new perspective on the world." Brer Rabbit paused. "You wouldn't—? Nah."

"Wouldn't what?" Brer Bear asked.

"Well, you wouldn't want to take over, would you? I mean, I know you've got family to feed, and you'd make a mighty fine watchbear. And a dollar a minute is nothing to sneeze at."

Brer Bear didn't much like the idea of hanging upside-down, but he liked the idea of making a dollar a minute. It wasn't long before Brer Bear let Brer Rabbit down, stuck his own leg through the loop, and took Brer Rabbit's place hanging upside-down from the tree. The branch hung so low that Brer Bear almost bumped his head on the ground as he dangled in the air.

"Enjoy yourself, Brer Bear," said Brer Rabbit. Then he ran to Brer Fox's house.

"Oh Brer Fox! Brer Fox! Wake up and I'll show you who's been stealing your peanuts," Brer Rabbit called from outside Brer Fox's window. Right away, Brer Fox got up and ran off to the patch with Brer Rabbit.

There they saw Brer Bear, hanging upside-down from the tree and grinning bigger than a hyena.

"Howdy, Brer Fox!" said Brer Bear. "I'm glad I could be—OWW!" Brer Bear didn't finish—Brer Fox had thwacked him on the behind.

"What'd you do that for? I'm only help—OUCH!" Brer Bear stopped again as Brer Fox swung his stick once more.

It went on like this for about half an hour. Every time Brer Bear tried to explain, Brer Fox thwacked him again. And every time Brer Fox thwacked him, Brer Bear tried even harder to explain.

While all this was going on, Brer Rabbit slipped away and hid in a nearby pond.

He knew that once the thwacking was over, Brer Bear would be coming after him. So he stayed in the pond until he heard Brer Bear furiously lumbering up the road.

Only Brer Rabbit's eyes poked out above the mud. Brer Bear thought he was a bullfrog.

"Howdy, Brer Bullfrog," grumbled Brer Bear. "You seen Brer Rabbit go by?"

"He just went by—CHUGARUMP!" said Brer Rabbit. "He went that way—CHUGARUMP!" pointing his eyes to the east.

"Mighty obliged, Brer Bullfrog," said Brer Bear. And off he lumbered.

Brer Rabbit stayed in the pond until Brer bear was well out of sight. Then he headed off the other way for home, laughing all the way.

Little Miss Muffet
  Sat on a tuffet,
Eating her curds and whey;
  Along came a spider,
Who sat down beside her,
  And frightened Miss Muffet away.

Jack and Jill went up the hill,
To fetch a pail of water;
Jack fell down, and broke his crown,
And Jill came tumbling after.

Hickory, dickory, dock!
The mouse ran up the clock;
The clock struck one,
And down he run,
Hickory, dickory, dock!

The Velveteen Rabbit

THERE WAS ONCE A VELVETEEN RABBIT, AND IN THE BEGINNING HE WAS REALLY SPLENDID. HE WAS FAT AND BUNCHY, AS A rabbit should be; his coat was spotted brown and white, he had real thread whiskers, and his ears were lined with pink sateen. On Christmas morning, when he sat wedged in the top of the Boy's stocking, with a sprig of holly between his paws, the effect was charming.

There were other things in the stocking, nuts and oranges and a toy engine, and chocolate almonds and a clockwork mouse, but the Rabbit was quite the best of all. For at least two hours the Boy loved him, and then Aunts and Uncles came to dinner, and there was a great rustling of tissue paper and unwrapping of parcels, and in the excitement of looking at all the new presents the Velveteen Rabbit was forgotten.

For a long time he lived in the toy cupboard or on the nursery floor, and no one thought very much about him. He was naturally shy, and being only made of velveteen, some of the more expensive toys quite snubbed him. The mechanical toys were very superior, and looked down upon everyone else; they were full of modern ideas, and pretended they were real. Between them all the poor little rabbit was made to feel himself very insignificant and commonplace, and the only person who was kind to him at all was the Skin Horse.

The Skin Horse had lived longer in the nursery than any of the others. He was so old that his brown coat was bald in patches and showed the seams underneath, and most of the hairs in his tail had been pulled out to string bead necklaces. He was wise, for he had seen a long succession of mechanical toys arrive to boast and swagger, and by-and-by break their mainsprings and pass away, and he knew that they were only toys, and would never turn into anything else. For nursery magic is very strange and wonderful, and only those playthings that are old and wise and experienced like the Skin Horse understand all about it.

"What is real?" asked the Rabbit one day, when they were lying side by side near the nursery fender, before Nana came to tidy the room. "Does it mean having things that buzz inside you and a stick-out handle?"

"Real isn't how you are made," said the Skin Horse. "It's a thing that happens to you. When a child loves you for a long, long time, not just to play with, but REALLY loves you, then you become Real."

"Does it hurt?" asked the Rabbit.

"Sometimes," said the Skin Horse, for he was always truthful. "When you are Real you don't mind being hurt."

"Does it happen all at once, like being wound up," he asked, "or bit by bit?"

"It doesn't happen all at once," said the Skin Horse. "You become. It takes a long time. That's why it doesn't often happen to people who break easily, or have sharp edges, or who have to be carefully kept. Generally, by the time you are Real, most of your hair has been loved off, and your eyes drop out and you get loose in the joints and very shabby. But these things don't matter at all, because once you are Real you can't be ugly, except to people who don't understand."

"I suppose you are Real?" said the Rabbit. And then he wished he had not said it, for he thought the Skin Horse might be sensitive. But the Skin Horse only smiled.

"The Boy's Uncle made me Real," he said. "That was a great many years ago; but once you are Real you can't become unreal again. It lasts for always."

The Rabbit sighed. He thought it would be a long time before this magic called Real happened to him. He longed to become Real, to know what it felt like; and yet the idea of growing shabby and losing his eyes and whiskers was rather sad. He wished that he could become it without these uncomfortable things happening to him.

There was a person called Nana who ruled the nursery. Sometimes she took no notice of the playthings laying about, and sometimes, for no reason whatsoever, she went swooping about like a great wind and hustled them away in cupboards.

One evening, when the Boy was going to bed, he couldn't find the china dog that always slept with him. Nana was in a hurry, and it was too much trouble to hunt for china dogs at bedtime, so she simply looked about her, and seeing that the toy cupboard door stood open, she made a swoop.

"Here," she said, "take your old Bunny! He'll do to sleep with you!" And she dragged the Rabbit out by the ear, and put him into the Boy's arms.

That night, and for many nights after, the velveteen Rabbit slept in the Boy's bed. At first he found it rather uncomfortable, for the Boy hugged him very tight, and sometimes he rolled over on him, and sometimes he pushed him so far under the pillow that the Rabbit could scarcely breathe. And he missed, too, those long moonlight hours in the nursery, when all the house was silent, and his talks with the Skin Horse. But very soon he grew to like it, for the Boy used to talk to him, and made nice tunnels for him under the bedclothes that he said were like the burrows the real rabbits lived in.

And when the Boy dropped off to sleep, the Rabbit would snuggle down close under his little warm chin and dream, with the Boy's hands clasped close round him all night long.

And so time went on, and the little Rabbit was very happy—so happy that he never noticed how his beautiful velveteen fur was getting shabbier and shabbier, and his tail was coming unsewn, and all the pink rubbed off his nose where the Boy had kissed him.

Spring came, and they had long days in the garden, for wherever the Boy went the Rabbit went, too. He had rides in the wheelbarrow, and picnics on the grass, and lovely fairy huts built for him under the raspberry canes behind the flower border. And once, when the Boy was called away suddenly to go out to tea, the Rabbit was left out on the lawn until long after dusk, and Nana had to come and look for him with the candle because the Boy couldn't go to sleep unless he was there. He was wet through with the dew and quite earthy from diving into the burrows the Boy had made for him in the flowerbed, and Nana grumbled as she rubbed him off with a corner of her apron.

"You must have your old Bunny!" she said. "Fancy all that fuss for a toy!"

The Boy sat up in bed and stretched out his hands.

"Give me my Bunny!" he said. "You mustn't say that. He isn't a toy. He's REAL!"

When the little Rabbit heard that he was happy, for he knew that what the Skin Horse had said was true at last. The nursery magic had happened to him, and he was a toy no longer. He was Real. The Boy himself had said it.

That night he was almost too happy to sleep, and so much love stirred in his little sawdust heart that it almost burst. And into his boot-button eyes, that had long ago lost their polish, there came a look of wisdom and beauty, so that even Nana noticed it next morning when she picked him up, and said, "I declare if that old Bunny hasn't got quite a knowing expression!"

That was a wonderful Summer!

Weeks passed, and the little Rabbit grew very old and shabby, but the Boy loved

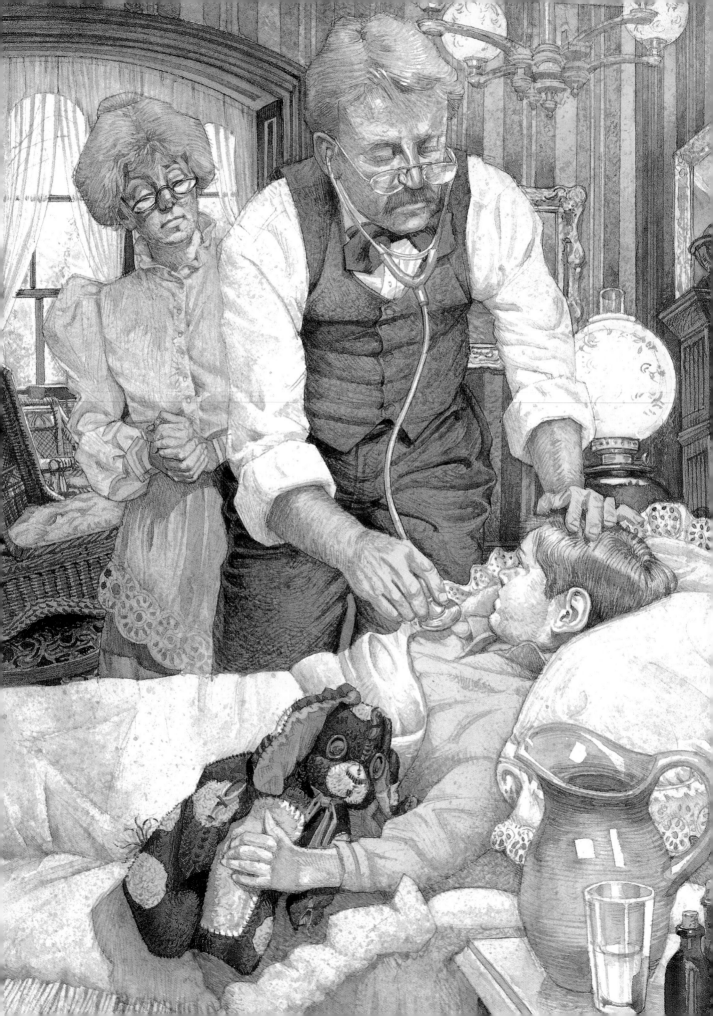

him just as much. He loved him so hard that he loved all his whiskers off, and the pink lining to his ears turned gray, and his brown spots faded. He even began to lose his shape, and scarcely looked like a rabbit any more, except to the Boy. To him he was always beautiful, and that was all that the little Rabbit cared about. He didn't mind how he looked to other people, because the nursery magic had made him Real, and when you are Real shabbiness doesn't matter.

And then, one day, the Boy was ill. His face grew very flushed, and he talked in his sleep, and his little body was so hot that it burned the Rabbit when he held him close. Strange people came and went in the nursery, and a light burned all night, and through it all the little Velveteen Rabbit lay there, hidden from sight under the bedclothes, and he never stirred, for he was afraid that if they found him someone might take him away, and he knew that the Boy needed him.

It was a long weary time, for the Boy was too ill to play, and the little Rabbit found it rather dull with nothing to do all day long. But he snuggled down patiently, and looked forward to the time when the Boy should be well again, and they would go out in the garden amongst the flowers and the butterflies and play splendid games in the raspberry thicket like they used to. All sorts of delightful things he planned, and while the Boy lay half asleep he crept up close to the pillow and whispered them in his ear. And presently the fever turned, and the Boy got better. He was able to sit up in bed and look at picture books, while the little Rabbit cuddled close at his side. And one day, they let him get up and dress.

It was a bright, sunny morning, and the windows stood wide open. They had carried the Boy out on to the balcony, wrapped in a shawl, and the little Rabbit lay tangled up among the bedclothes, thinking.

The Boy was going to the seaside tomorrow. Everything was arranged, and now it only remained to carry out the doctor's orders. They talked about it all, while the little Rabbit lay under the bedclothes, with just his head peeping out, and listened. The room was to be disinfected, and all the books and toys that the Boy had played with in bed must be burnt.

"Hurrah!" thought the little Rabbit. "Tomorrow we shall go to the seaside!" For the Boy had often talked of the seaside, and he wanted very much to see the big waves coming in, and the tiny crabs, and the sandcastles.

Just then Nana caught sight of him.

"How about this old Bunny?" she asked.

"That?" said the doctor. "Why, it's a mass of scarlet fever germs!—Burn it at once. What? Nonsense! Get him a new one. He mustn't have that any more!"

And so the little rabbit was put into a sack with the old picture books and a lot of rubbish, and carried out to the end of the garden behind the fowl-house. That was a fine place to make a bonfire, only the gardener was too busy just then to attend to it. He had the potatoes to dig and the green peas to gather, but the next morning he promised to come quite early and burn the whole lot.

That night the Boy slept in a different bedroom, and he had a new bunny to sleep with him. It was a splendid bunny, all white plush with real glass eyes, but the Boy was too excited to care very much about it. For tomorrow he was going to the seaside, and that in itself was such a wonderful thing that he could think of nothing else.

And while the Boy was asleep, dreaming of the seaside, the little Rabbit lay among the old picture books in the corner behind the fowl-house, and he felt very lonely. The sack had been left untied, and so by wriggling a bit he was able to get his head through the opening and look out. He was shivering a little, for he had always been used to sleeping in a proper bed, and by this time his coat had worn so thin and thread-bare from hugging that it was no longer any protection to him. He thought of those long sunlit hours in the garden—how happy they were—and a

great sadness came over him. He thought of the Skin Horse, so wise and gentle, and all that he had told him. Of what use was it to be loved and lose one's beauty and become Real if it all ended like this? And a tear, a real tear, trickled down his little shabby velvet nose and fell to the ground.

And then a strange thing happened. For where the tear had fallen, a flower grew out of the ground, a mysterious flower, not at all like any that grew in the garden. It had slender green leaves the color of emeralds, and in the center of the leaves a blossom like a golden cup. It was so beautiful that the little Rabbit forgot to cry, and just lay there watching it. And presently the blossom opened, and out of it there stepped a fairy.

She was quite the loveliest fairy in the whole world. Her dress was of pearls and dewdrops, and there were flowers around her neck and in her hair, and her face was like the most perfect flower of all. And she came close to the little rabbit and gathered him up in her arms and kissed him on his velveteen nose that was all damp from crying.

"I am the nursery magic Fairy," she said. "I take care of all the playthings that the children have loved. When they are old and worn out and the children don't need them anymore, then I come and take them away with me and turn them into Real."

"Wasn't I Real before?" asked the little Rabbit.

"You were Real to the Boy," the Fairy said, "because he loved you. Now you shall be Real to everyone."

And she held the little rabbit close in her arms and flew with him into the wood.

In the open glade between the tree-trunks the wild rabbits danced with their shadows on the velvet grass, but when they saw the Fairy they all stopped dancing and stood round in a ring to stare at her.

"I've brought you a new playfellow," the Fairy said. "You must be very kind to him and teach him all he needs to know in Rabbitland, for he is going to live with you for ever and ever!"

And she kissed the little Rabbit again and put him down on the grass.

"Run and play, little Rabbit!" she said.

But the little Rabbit sat quite still for a moment and never moved. He did not know that when the Fairy kissed him that last time she had changed him altogether. And he might have sat there a long time, too shy to move, if just then something hadn't tickled his nose, and before he thought what he was doing he lifted his hind toe to scratch it.

And he found that he actually had hind legs! Instead of dingy velveteen he had brown fur, soft and shiny, his ears twitched by themselves, and his whiskers were so long that they brushed the grass. He gave one leap and the joy of using those hind legs was so great that he went springing about the turf on them, jumping sideways and whirling round as the others did, and he grew so excited that when at last he did stop to look for the fairy she had gone.

Autumn passed and winter, and in the spring, when the days grew warm and sunny, the Boy went out to play in the wood behind the house. And while he was playing, two rabbits crept out from the bracken and peeped at him. One of them was brown all over, but the other had strange markings under his fur, as though long ago he had been spotted, and the spots still showed through. And about his little soft nose and his round black eyes there was something familiar, so that the Boy thought to himself:

"Why, he looks just like my old Bunny that was lost when I had scarlet fever!"

But he never knew that it really was his own Bunny, come back to look at the child who had first helped him to be real.

THE END

The Fox
and the Crow

A fox spied a crow sitting on a branch of a tall tree with a golden piece of cheese in her beak. The fox, who was both clever and hungry, quickly thought of a plan to get the cheese away from the crow.

Pretending to notice the crow for the first time, the fox exclaimed, "My, what a beautiful bird! I must say that is the most elegant black plumage I have ever seen. Look how it shines in the sun. Simply magnificent!"

The crow was flattered by all this talk about her feathers. She listened to every sugary word the fox spoke.

The fox continued, "I must say that this is the most beautiful bird in the world. But I wonder, can such a stunning bird have an equally splendid voice? That," said the cunning fox, "would be too much to ask."

The crow, wanting the fox to hear her voice, opened her beak to let out an ear-piercing "CAW!" As she did so, the cheese tumbled out of her mouth and was gobbled up instantly by the fox.

NEVER TRUST A FLATTERER.

Mowgli's Adventure

Mowgli, the man-cub, lived a wonderful life among the wolves. When he was not playing, he sat out in the sun and slept, and then ate and slept again. When he felt dirty or hot, he swam in the forest pools.

Baloo the Bear was delighted to have Mowgli as a pupil, for Mowgli was a quick learner. Baloo taught young Mowgli all kinds of things, like the hunting-calls, and how to climb, and how to get honey without being stung.

"I am teaching Mowgli the master Words," Baloo told Bagheera the Black Panther one day. "He can now ask for help from all the Jungle-People, if he remembers the words."

"I am more likely to give help than to ask for it," said Bagheera, admiring his sharp talons. "Still, I should like to hear them."

Baloo called to Mowgli, who was sulking under a tree. Baloo had to be stern when he taught, for the Law of the Jungle is serious business. That day, Mowgli had grown tired of his teacher's proddings.

"I come for Bagheera, not for you, fat old Baloo!" grumbled Mowgli.

"I do not care," said Baloo, although he was hurt. "Tell Bagheera the Mater Words. First for the birds."

"We are of one blood, you and I," Mowgli whistled and chirped.

"Very good!" said Baloo. "Now for the Snake-People."

"We are of one blood, you and I," Mowgli answered with a great hissing. Then he jumped on Bagheera's back and made faces at Baloo.

"One of these days," Mowgli exclaimed, 'I will have my own tribe, and we will throw branches and dirt at you, Baloo."

"Whoof!" Baloo's big paw scooped Mowgli from Bagheera's shoulders. "Mowgli, have you been talking with the Monkey-People? Answer me honestly!"

"One day, after you scolded me, the gray apes came

down from the trees and said they wanted to be my friends," Mowgli sniffed.

Baloo's voice rumbled. "Man-cub, I have taught you the laws of all the Jungle-People, except for the Monkey-People. This is because they have no law. They are foolish boasters, and they are forbidden."

Far up in the trees, a group of monkeys chattered. One told the others how he had seen Mowgli weave sticks into a shelter. This was something the Monkey-People did not know how to do. Then one of them had an idea: if they captured Mowgli, they could make him their teacher.

When it was time for a nap, Mowgli lay down between his friends and fell asleep. The next thing he knew, he felt hands on his legs and arms—strong, hairy hands. Then he was staring down through swaying branches. The monkeys howled with triumph as they swung away with Mowgli.

The flight of the Monkey-People was incredible. The monkeys swung recklessly from tree to tree, up to a hundred feet above the ground. Two of them held Mowgli under his arms as they went. Mowgli was both sick and giddy from their speed. From the tops of the trees, he could see for miles across the Jungle.

As exciting as this was, Mowgli became angry. More than once, he thought the monkeys would drop him. Looking up and away, Mowgli saw Chil the Kite soaring nearby. Mowgli whistled, and Chil dropped down to investigate.

"We are of one blood, you and I!" Mowgli called, using the Master Words for the birds.

"Who are you, friend?" whistled Chil.

"I am Mowgli. Tell Baloo and Bagheera where I go!" Mowgli shrieked as the monkeys dipped back below the treetops. Chil rocked on his wings and watched.

Meanwhile, Bagheera and Baloo had lost sight of Mowgli.

"Whoo!" moaned Baloo. "Put dead bats on my head! I am miserable!" He clasped his head and rolled on the ground.

"You are acting like a porcupine!" scolded

Bagheera. "Let us think of a plan."

"I am a fool!" said Baloo, sitting up. "The Monkey-People do not fear us, because we cannot move through the trees. But there is one who they do fear. Let us find Kaa."

Baloo and Bagheera soon found Kaa the Python stretched out on a warm ledge, looking shiny and splendid with the thirty feet of his body twisted into great muscular loops.

Baloo stepped up to Kaa and sat down. "Good hunting!" cried Baloo.

"Good hunting to us all," the snake answered sleepily. "Is there game afoot?"

"We are hunting," Baloo said casually.

"Then allow me to come with you. I am so big now that a branch snapped during my last hunt. My tail was not wrapped around the tree, and the noise of my falling woke the Monkey-People. They called me evil names."

"Yes. Like . . . footless, yellow earth-worm," said Bagheera under his whiskers, as though he were trying to remember something.

"Ssssss!

They call me that?" demanded Kaa.

"Oh, yes," said Bagheera.

Then Bagheera cut to the point: "The trouble is this, Kaa.
Those pickers of palm leaves have stolen away our man-cub."

"He is the best and boldest, and my own pupil," said Baloo. "We
love him, Kaa."

"I, too, know what love is," said Kaa. "These monkeys are foolish, and careless. We must remind them who their masters are."

"Look up!" cried a voice above them. The three looked up and
saw Chil swooping overhead.

"I have seen a man-cub," whistled Chil. "He asked me to find
you. The monkeys have taken him to the Cold Lairs." Few of the
Jungle-People went to the Cold Lairs. It was an ancient, deserted city,
buried deep in the Jungle.

"Thank you, Chil!" cried Baloo. The kite wheeled away into the afternoon sun.

"We must go quickly," said Bagheera. With that, he set off into the Jungle at
a brisk canter. Kaa matched his speed, slithering powerfully along the ground.
Baloo soon fell behind. Panting, he promised to catch up as soon as he could.

The monkeys dragged Mowgli into the Cold Lairs in the late afternoon.
The monkeys called this their city, yet they did not know how the buildings
were meant to be used. They would sit in the king's throne-room and
scratch for fleas. Or they would explore, but would immediately
forget where they had just been. The city's battlements were
tumbled down, and vines hung from the windows of the now-
roofless palace. But even in ruin, it was still splendid.

The monkeys put Mowgli on a white marble
terrace. He could not help laughing as

they began to tell him how wise they were. The monkeys gathered by the hundreds to listen to each other.

"We are great!" they shouted. "We are the most wonderful people of the Jungle! We all say so, so it must be true!" The monkeys shouted and danced all afternoon, swinging each other by the arms. Mowgli kept silent, sure that they were all crazy.

Daylight faded. As the monkeys lounged around him in circles fifty or sixty deep, jabbering, Mowgli wondered how the night would end. Suddenly he heard Bagheera's light feet on the terrace. Without warning, the black panther began striking left and right at the monkeys with his powerful paws. There were howls of fright and rage. Then Bagheera tripped on the wriggling bodies beneath him.

"There is only one! Attack him!" screamed the monkeys.

Biting and pulling, a mass of monkeys closed over Bagheera. Mowgli thrashed as six monkeys pulled him away. They tossed him into a ruined summerhouse, through a hole in the domed roof, where the entrance was blocked and he could not climb out.

Then from another wall rose a bear's roar. Old Baloo had arrived! He jumped on a trio of monkeys and gave them a big bear-hug. With a whoosh, the air rushed from their lungs and they collapsed. Baloo waded into the next wave, throwing monkeys this way and that.

But the monkeys kept coming. Soon the panther was trapped in a corner, and the bear was covered by furious Monkey-People. Mowgli's heart beat in his throat.

Then, out of nowhere, came Kaa. A python can strike a blow with his head, like a battering-ram. A python four or five feet long can knock a man down. Kaa was thirty feet long, a half-ton of pure muscle. Kaa delivered his first blow to the crowd around Baloo. Monkeys flew everywhere.

The monkeys had feared Kaa for generations, so they scattered, chattering with terror. Baloo sighed with relief, and helped Mowgli from his prison.

But Kaa was not done. He opened his mouth and spoke one long, hissing word. Up in the trees, on the walls, and on the broken buildings, the monkeys froze where they were. It was eerily silent in the Cold Lairs.

The python turned to look at Mowgli.

"We are of one blood, you and I," said Mowgli respectfully. "If you are ever hungry, I will hunt for you, O great Kaa. I will repay the debt I owe to you."

"Thanks, Little Brother," said Kaa, his eyes twinkling. "You have a brave heart and a courteous tongue. Now it grows late. But before we go, I must attend to one last piece of business."

Kaa glided to the center of the terrace. He snapped his jaws.

"Now Monkey-People, begins the Dance of Kaa. You will not forget that Kaa is your master!"

Humming one note, the python turned in a big circle, weaving his head from left to right. Then he began making loops and figure eights. Then came soft, oozy triangles that melted into squares and other fantastic shapes. Kaa never stopped moving, never stopped his hum. Mowgli watched in wonder.

"Monkey-People, can you move?" asked the voice of Kaa.

The monkeys were frozen, their eyes glazed. "No, O Kaa!" they whispered in unison.

"Good!" said Kaa. "Come one pace toward me."

Hypnotized, all the monkeys took one step forward. Baloo and

Bagheera felt Kaa's magic, too, and swayed on their feet. Mowgli put his hands on their shoulders, to wake them. Together, the three of them turned away. As they left the Cold Lairs, they heard Kaa command the monkeys never to bother the man-cub again.

When they were some distance away, they sat down. Mowgli saw that Baloo and Bagheera were tired and sore.

"I was bad to mock you, and disobey your wishes," said Mowgli sorrowfully.

"Yes, you have been bad. Feel sorrowful, for that is the Law," said Bagheera. Mowgli felt terrible, and stared at the ground.

After a few moments, Baloo said: "There. That is enough. We are satisfied, Mowgli. Now give me a smile." Mowgli slowly raised his head, and saw that his teacher was beaming with love.

"Come," said Bagheera, "jump on my back, Little Brother, and we will go home."

Mowgli did, and laid his head down on Bagheera's shoulder. He drifted off and slept deeply, even when his friend put him down in his own cave.

"Pussy-cat, pussy-cat, where have you been?"
"I've been to London to look at the Queen."
"Pussy-cat, pussy-cat, what did you there?"
"I frightened a little mouse under the chair."

Three blind mice!
See how they run!
They all ran after the farmer's wife,
Who cut off their tails with a carving knife.
Did you ever see such a sight
in all your life
As three blind mice?

Jack be nimble, Jack be quick,
Jack jump over the candlestick.

Brier Rose

In days long past, there was a couple, a king and queen, who spent each day in their magnificent palace wishing for only one thing, a child. Years came and went, and yet they were never blessed with a child.

A frog appeared to the queen as she was bathing one day. He came to her and said, "The wish of the great king and queen shall be granted. In the year to come, you shall bear a daughter."

The queen thought little of what the frog had said, as she was sure that she would never have a child. But the frog had spoken the truth and within the year, the people of the kingdom were celebrating the birth of the king and queen's daughter, the princess. The king and queen were so elated at the arrival of the child that they decided to hold a grand feast to celebrate. They invited what seemed to be the whole of the kingdom. This included thirteen wise women. Unfortunately, there were only twelve golden plates from which they could eat. Therefore, one of them would be unable to attend.

The feast was celebrated with great jubilation, and as it was nearing the end, the twelve wise women came forward to bequeath their gifts to the infant princess. She was given such gifts as beauty, wealth, and virtue. As the twelfth wise woman was about to give the child her gift, the thirteenth woman, who had not been included

in the celebration, burst into the room, seeking revenge. The evil woman hovered over the child and placed an evil curse upon her, "Upon the dawning of her fifteenth year, the princess shall prick her finger on a spindle and die!" With that, she turned and left all of the people of the kingdom standing there in horrified silence. The twelfth wise woman stepped forward to give the child her gift. While she did not have the power to undo the evil curse, she could change the outcome.

"Upon pricking her finger on the spindle, the princess shall fall into a peaceful slumber of one hundred years, but will not die."

The king was still not satisfied and was determined to do all that he could to protect his precious daughter. All spindles in the kingdom were ordered destroyed and he watched over the years as his daughter grew into a beautiful young woman. Each of the gifts of the wise women were apparent in the kind and gentle ways of the princess.

On the day of her fifteenth birthday, the princess found herself alone in the palace, the king and queen away for the day. And so the princess explored the many rooms and chambers of the palace that she had never before seen. She soon came to the tower, and climbed to the top of a tall, winding staircase that ended at a small door. She unlocked the door with a key that sat in the

rusty lock, and found a simple

old woman, spinning flax upon a spindle.

"What is that you are doing?" she questioned the

old woman.

"Why, I'm spinning."

"What is that?" asked the princess, as she reached out and touched the bobbing

spindle. And with that, the princess fell upon the bed that sat beside her in a deep,

deep sleep. It did not take long before this silent slumber had reached the rest of the

kingdom. The king and the queen, the horses in the stables, the birds of the sky, all

fell into the same deep sleep as the princess. All became quiet and still. There were

no fires or winds—no sound or tremble.

A brier hedge began to grow all along the walls of the great castle, and it soon

covered so great an area that the palace could no longer be seen. The princess

became known as the beautiful sleeping Brier Rose, and her story was passed from

town to town and country to country. Many princes came with the hopes of saving

the princess and winning her heart. But the brier hedge was far too strong and

treacherous to get through.

Many years had passed since the curse had fallen upon the kingdom, when a

prince came to the country and heard the tale of the beautiful princess, asleep

within the brier-covered walls of the castle. Many tried to warn the prince against

trying to save the princess. No man had ever made it past the thorns of the brier.

But the young prince showed no fear, and set out to save the beautiful Brier Rose.

It was on the last day of the hundredth year of her slumber that the prince set forth to save the princess. As the prince approached the palace, he found beautiful blossoms in the place of the brier's menacing thorns. He walked easily through its gates, only to find the entire kingdom fast asleep. As he looked around, he could see everyone from the king's cook to the fly on the wall sleeping peacefully. Still, he did not see the princess.

After much searching, he came to the tower. He climbed the staircase and opened the door, and there was the princess. She lay silently on the same bed that had held her for one hundred years. Her beauty was so overwhelming that the prince could not bear to take his eyes off her for even a moment. He walked to her bedside, leaned down, and placed a gentle kiss upon her lips. Slowly, Brier Rose's eyes opened and she was freed from the curse.

Together they walked down from the tower and looked around the palace. All around, the kingdom was waking from its extended rest. Soon, the horses, the hounds, the pigeons, and even the flies on the wall were awake.

Brier Rose and the handsome price soon wed, and were celebrated with much joy. Together, they lived happily for all the days of their lives.

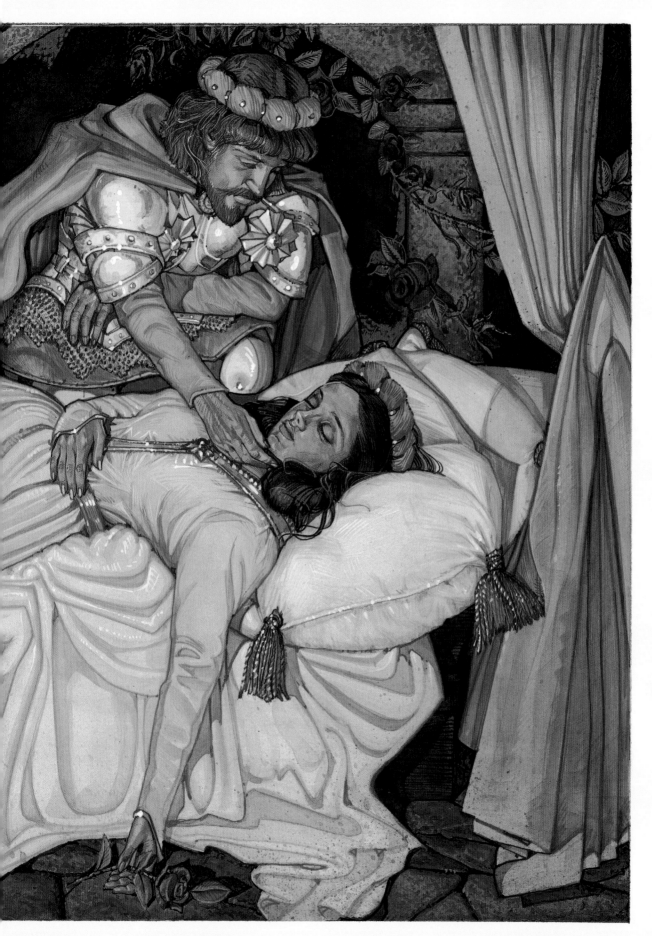

The Tortoise and the Hare

The hare couldn't understand how the tortoise ever accomplished anything.

"Tell me, tell me!" demanded the hare as he hopped circles around the tortoise. "How do you get things done? You move so slowly that you hardly move at all. Just look at me—look at me—I cover lots of ground every day."

To prove it, the hare sprinted across the field and back again before the tortoise could open his mouth.

"Well . . ." began the tortoise as he considered his answer, "it's like this . . . First of all, I find it much better to plan ahead and then—"

"No time for this! No time!" interrupted the hare. And in a flash, he was gone. A few days later, the hare happened to meet the tortoise on a mossy rock.

"Hey there, Mr. Tortoise!" shouted the hare, appearing suddenly and giving the tortoise a terrible scare. "If you don't watch out, somebody's going to make soup out of you."

"Oh," replied the tortoise, poking his head out of his shell, "you're just mocking me. Besides . . . I don't believe—"

But the hare was impatient. "I think what you need is some exercise. It'll start your heart pumping. It'll get your blood moving. Try it! You'll see! You'll see!"

"Exercise?" said the tortoise. "Let me think a moment . . . Hmm . . . By exercise, do you mean—"

"A race!" blurted the hare. "I challenge you to a race."

And before the tortoise could reply, the date was set. On the morning of the race, everyone turned out to witness the contest of the season. The owl had selected a fair course the night before, and the lion and the frog agreed to judge the race and announce the winner.

The tortoise and the hare stood side by side at the starting line. The race was about to begin. The crowd held its breath. A crow, sitting in a nearby tree, dropped a twig, signaling the start. When the twig hit the ground, the racers were off.

The shouts and croaks and caws and barks of the crowd were deafening, but the hare was already too far ahead to hear them. The tortoise moved along as fast as he could, which is to say, not very fast at all. But soon he, too, was well away from the starting line.

When the hare reached the halfway mark, he turned to look behind him. The tortoise was nowhere in sight. It was almost lunchtime, and the hare thought about making a salad to celebrate his certain victory. He went off in search of carrots and lettuce and whatever else he might find.

Meanwhile, the tortoise plodded along, slowly closing the gap between himself and the hare. The whole time he kept in his mind the thought of crossing the finish line.

The hare had gathered a huge amount of salad greens for his victory salad, and even went to the trouble of finding tender blossoms. When he had finished the last of his lunch, he returned to the track and dashed a little farther ahead. But the sun was high and hot, and the hare was drowsy from such a big meal. Once again he left the track, this time in search of some shade.

Little did he know that the tortoise was behind him, just around the bend.

"There's one thing I have to give the tortoise credit for," thought the hare, as he drifted off to sleep. "Since he carries his house with him, he can get shade whenever he wants."

The tortoise pressed onward, not even realizing that he was passing the hare. "He's nowhere in sight," the tortoise thought, "but the race isn't over until it's over."

Like the hare, the tortoise was also feeling tired from the sun, but he kept his

goal in mind. "One thing I have to give the hare credit for," he said to himself. "At least he doesn't have to carry his home with him wherever he goes. No wonder he can move so fast."

The tortoise kept moving, and the hare dreamed about victory.

A while later, the tortoise began to hear the friendly sounds of animals chirping, cawing, and growling, and he realized that he was nearing the finish line. As he cleared the top of a hill, he could see the crowd at the bottom. The crowd saw him, too, and began to cheer.

In his dreams, the hare thought the cheers were for him, but suddenly he awoke and realized the race was not yet won. He jumped up and dashed for the finish line. He reached the top of the last hill just in time to see the tortoise win.

SLOW AND STEADY WINS THE RACE.

Mr. Toad's Wild Ride

It was a bright morning in the early part of summer. The Mole and the Water Rat were finishing breakfast in the parlor, when a heavy knock sounded at the door. The Mole went to attend the summons, and the Rat heard him utter a cry of surprise, fling the parlor door open, and announce, "Mr. Badger!"

The Badger strode heavily into the room. "The hour has come!" he said.

"What hour?" asked the Rat uneasily.

"Why, Toad's hour! The hour of Toad! I said I would take him in hand as soon as the winter was well over, and I'm going to take him in hand today!"

"Of course!" cried the Mole delightedly. "I remember now! We'll teach him to be a sensible Toad!"

"This very morning," continued the Badger, "another new motor-car will arrive at Toad Hall. You two animals must accompany me instantly."

They reached Toad Hall to find a shiny new motor-car standing in front of the house. As they neared the door it was flung open, and Mr. Toad came swaggering down the steps, drawing on his gauntleted gloves.

"Hullo! come on, you fellows!" he cried. "You're just in time to come with me for a jolly—for a—er—jolly..."

His hearty accents faltered and fell away as he noticed the stern look of his silent friends. The Badger strode up the steps. "Take him inside," he said to his companions.

"Now then!" he said to the Toad, "First of all, take those ridiculous things off!"

"Shan't!" replied Toad, with great spirit. "What is the meaning of this gross outrage?"

"Take them off him, then, you two," ordered the Badger.

They laid Toad out on the floor, kicking and calling names. The Rat sat on him, the Mole got his motor-clothes off, and they stood him up again. Now that he was merely Toad, and no longer the Terror of the Highway, he giggled feebly and looked from one to the other appealingly.

"You knew it must come to this, sooner or later, Toad," the Badger explained severely. "You're getting us animals a bad name by your furious driving and your smashes and your rows with the police. Now, I'll make one more effort to bring you to reason." He took Toad firmly by the arm, led him into the smoking room and closed the door behind them.

After some three-quarters of an hour the door opened, and the Badger reappeared solemnly leading a very dejected Toad. "There's only one more thing to be done," continued the gratified Badger, "Toad, repeat before your friends here what you admitted to me in the smoking room. First, you are sorry for what you've done, and you see the folly of it all?"

There was a long, long pause but at last Toad spoke.

"No!" he said, a little sullenly, but stoutly; "I'm NOT sorry. And it wasn't folly at all! It was simply glorious!"

"What?" cried the Badger, greatly scandalized. "Then you don't promise never to touch a motor-car again?"

"Certainly not!" replied Toad. "On the contrary, I faithfully promise that the very first motor-car I see, *poop-poop!* Off I go!"

"Very well, then," said the Badger. "Since you won't yield, we'll try what force can do. Take him upstairs, you two, and lock him up in his bedroom."

"It's for your own good, Toady, you know," said the Rat kindly, as Toad, kicking and struggling, was hauled up the stairs by his two faithful friends. "Think what fun we shall all have together, just as we used to, when you've quite got over this!"

"We'll take great care of everything for you till you're well, Toad," said the Mole. "And we'll see your money isn't wasted, as it has been," added the Mole, turning the key on him.

They descended the stair, Toad shouting abuse at them

through the keyhole, and the three friends met in conference.

"I've never seen Toad so determined," said the Badger. "He must never be left an instant unguarded."

Each animal took it in turns to sleep in Toad's room at night, and they divided the day up between them. At first Toad was undoubtedly very trying. He would arrange bedroom chairs in rude resemblance of a motor-car and crouch on them staring fixedly ahead, making uncouth and ghastly noises until, turning a complete somersault, he would lie amidst the ruins of the chairs. But as time passed, he grew apparently languid and depressed.

One fine morning the Rat went upstairs to relieve Badger. "Toad's still in bed," Badger told him as he was leaving. "Can't get much out of him. Now, you look out, Rat! When Toad's quiet and submissive, then there's sure to be something up."

"How are you today, old chap?" inquired the Rat.

He had to wait some minutes for an answer. At last a feeble voice replied, "Thank you so much, dear Ratty! So good of you to inquire! Do not trouble about me. I hate being a burden to my friends, and I do not expect to be one much longer."

"Well," said the Rat heartily. "You've been a fine bother to us, and I'm glad to hear it's going to stop. I tell you, I'd take any trouble on earth for you, if only you'd be a sensible animal."

"If I thought that, Ratty," murmured Toad, more feebly than ever, "then I would beg you—for the last time, probably—to step round to the village and fetch the doctor."

"Why, what do you want a doctor for?" inquired the Rat, examining him. He certainly lay very still, and his voice was weaker and his manner much changed. "O, he must be really bad!" the Rat said to himself, as he hurried from the room, not forgetting, however, to lock the door behind him.

The Toad, who had hopped lightly out of bed as soon as he heard the key turned, watched eagerly from the window till Ratty disappeared. Then, knotting the sheets from his bed together and tying one end round the window, he scrambled out, and marched off lightheartedly, whistling a merry tune.

It was a gloomy luncheon for Rat when the Badger and the Mole returned. "He did it awfully well," said the crestfallen Rat.

"He did YOU awfully well!" rejoined Badger hotly. "Toad's got clear away for the time, and the worst of it is, he'll be so conceited with his cleverness that he may commit any folly."

Meanwhile, Toad, gay and irresponsible, was walking briskly along the high road, some miles from home. He had reached a little town, when an only too familiar sound made him start and fall a-trembling all over. The *poop-poop* drew nearer and nearer. The car could be heard to turn into the inn-yard and come to a stop. Waiting eagerly for a time, at last he could stand it no longer. "There cannot be any harm," he said to himself, "in my only just LOOKING at it!"

The car stood in the middle of the yard, quite unattended. Toad walked slowly round it.

"I wonder," he said to himself presently, "if this sort of car STARTS easily?"

The next moment, hardly knowing how it came about, he found he had hold of the handle and was turning it. As the familiar sound broke forth, the old passion completely mastered him. As if in a dream he found himself, somehow, seated in the driver's seat, pulling the lever and swinging the car round the yard and out through the archway. He increased his pace and leapt forth on the high road, only conscious that he was Toad once more, Toad the Terror, the Lord of the Loan Trail. He chanted as he flew, and the car responded with sonorous drone; as he sped he knew not what might come to him.

"To my mind," observed the Chairman of the Bench of Magistrates cheerfully, "the ONLY difficulty is, how we can possibly make it sufficiently hot for the ruffian whom

we see cowering in the dock before us. Let me see: he has been found guilty, on the clearest evidence, first, of stealing a valuable motor-car; secondly, of driving to the public danger; and, thirdly, of gross impertinence to the rural police. Mr. Clerk, will you tell us, please, what is the very stiffest penalty we can impose for each of these offenses?"

The Clerk scratched his nose with his pen. "Supposing you were to say twelve months for the theft, three years for the furious driving, and fifteen years for cheeking the police—those figures, if added together correctly, tot up to nineteen years."

"First-rate!" said the Chairman.

"So you had better make it a round twenty years and be on the safe side," concluded the Clerk.

"An excellent suggestion!" said the Chairman approvingly. "Prisoner! It's going to be twenty years for you this time. Mind, if you appear before us again, we shall have to deal with you very seriously!" On this note, the brutal minions of the law loaded Toad with chains, and dragged him from the courthouse to the door of the grimmest dungeon.

"Oddsbodikins!" said the sergeant of police, "Rouse thee, old loon, and take over from us this vile Toad. The gaoler nodded grimly, laying his withered hand on the shoulder of the miserable Toad. The rusty key creaked in the lock, the great door clanged behind them.

When Toad found himself immured in a dank dungeon, and knew that all the grim darkness of a medieval fortress lay between him and the outer world of sunshine and well-metalled high roads where he had lately been so happy, he flung himself on the floor, and shed bitter tears. "O clever, intelligent Rat and sensible Mole! What sound judgments, what a knowledge of men and matters you possess!" With lamentations such as these he passed his days and nights for several weeks, refusing his meals from the grim gaoler.

The gaoler had a daughter who was good-hearted, and assisted her father in the lighter duties. She was particularly fond of animals, and took pity on the misery of Toad, saying, "Father! I can't bear to see that poor beast so unhappy. You let me have the managing of him. I'll make him eat from my hand, and sit up, and do all sorts of things."

Her father replied that she could do what she liked with him. He was tired of Toad, and his sulks and airs. So that day she went on her errand of mercy, and knocked at the door of Toad's cell.

"Now, cheer up, Toad," she said, "and sit up and dry your eyes and be a sensible animal." She carried a tray, with a cup of fragrant tea steaming on it, and a plate piled up with very hot buttered toast. The smell of that buttered toast simply talked to Toad. He sat up on end, dried his eyes, sipped his tea, and munched his toast, and soon began talking freely about himself.

The gaoler's daughter saw that the talk was doing him as much good as the tea and encouraged him to go on. She listened to him until it was time for bed and, when she said good night, having filled his water-jug and shaken up his straw for him, Toad was very much the same sanguine, self-satisfied animal that he had been of old.

They had many interesting talks together, after that, as the dreary days went on, and the gaoler's daughter grew very sorry for Toad.

One morning the girl was very thoughtful, and answered at random, and did not seem to Toad to be paying proper attention to his witty sayings and sparkling comments.

"Toad," she said presently, "listen, please. I have an aunt who is a washerwoman."

"There, there," said Toad, graciously and affably, "Never mind; think no more about it. I have several aunts that ought to be washerwomen."

"Do be quiet a minute Toad," the girl said. "She does the washing for all the prisoners in this castle. Now, this is what occurs to me: you're very rich—at least you're always telling me so—and she's very poor. A few pounds wouldn't make any difference to you, and it would mean a lot to her. Now, I think if she were properly approached, she would let you have her dress and bonnet and you could escape from the castle as the official washerwoman. You're very alike in many respects—particularly about the figure."

"We're NOT," said the Toad in a huff. "I have a very elegant figure—for what I am."

"So has my aunt," replied the girl, "for what SHE is. But have it your own way. You horrid, proud, ungrateful animal, when I'm sorry for you and trying to help you!"

Honest Toad was always ready to admit himself in the wrong. "You are a good, kind, clever girl," he said. "And I am indeed a proud and stupid toad. Introduce me to your worthy aunt, and I have no doubt that the excellent lady and I will be able to arrange something."

Next evening, the girl ushered her aunt into Toad's cell. In return for his cash, Toad received a cotton print gown, an apron, a shawl, and a rusty black bonnet; the only stipulation the old lady made being that she should be gagged and bound and dumped down in a corner. By this not very convincing artifice, she explained, aided by picturesque fiction which she could supply herself, she hoped to retain her situation, in spite of the suspicious appearance of things.

Toad was delighted with the suggestion. It would enable him to leave the prison in some style, and with his reputation for being a desperate and dangerous fellow untarnished. "Take off that coat and waistcoat of yours; you're fat enough as it is," said the girl.

Shaking with laughter, she proceeded to "hook-and-eye" him into the cotton print gown, arranged the shawl with a professional fold, and tied the strings of the rusty bonnet under his chin.

"You're the very image of her," she giggled, "only I'm sure you never looked half so respectable in all your life before. Now, good-bye, Toad, and good luck. Go straight down the way you came up."

Toad set forth cautiously but he was soon agreeably surprised to find how easy everything was made for him. The washerwoman's squat figure in its familiar cotton print seemed a passport for every barred door and grim gateway.

It seemed hours before he crossed the last courtyard, but at last he heard the wicket-gate in the great outer door click behind him, felt the fresh air of the outer world upon his anxious brow, and knew that he was free!

Dizzy with the easy success of his daring exploit, he walked quickly towards the lights of the town, not knowing in the least what he should do next. As he walked along, considering, his attention was caught by some red and green lights a little way off. "Aha!" he thought, "this is a piece of luck! A railway station is the thing I want most in the whole world at this moment."

He made his way to the station accordingly, consulted a time-table, and found that a train, bound more or less in the direction of his home, was due to start in half-an-hour. "More luck!" said Toad, his spirits rising rapidly, and went off to the booking-office to buy his ticket.

He gave the name of the station nearest to Toad Hall, and mechanically put his fingers, in search of the necessary money, where his waistcoat pocket should have been. But here he found the cotton gown, which turned all muscular strivings to water; while other travelers, forming up in a line behind, waited with impatience.

To his horror he recollected that he had left both coat and waistcoat behind him in his cell. In his misery, he made one desperate effort to carry the thing off, and, with a return to his fine old manner, he said, "Look here! I find I've left my purse behind. Just give me that ticket, and I'll send the money on tomorrow. I'm well known in these parts."

The clerk stared at him and the rusty black bonnet a moment, and then he laughed. "I should think you were pretty well known in these parts," he said. "You've tried this game on often. Stand away from the window, please, madam; you're obstructing the other passengers!"

Baffled and full of despair, Toad wandered blindly down the platform where the train was standing, and tears trickled down each side of his nose. Very soon his escape would be discovered, the hunt would be up, he would be caught, and dragged back again to prison. What was to be done? As he pondered, he found himself opposite the engine, which was being oiled and wiped by its affectionate driver.

"Hullo, mother!" said the engine-driver, "What's the trouble? You don't look particularly cheerful."

"O, sir!" said Toad, crying afresh, "I am a poor unhappy washerwoman, and I've lost all my money, and can't pay for a ticket, and I must get home tonight somehow, and whatever I am to do I don't know. O dear, O dear!"

"That's a bad business, indeed," said the engine-driver reflectively. "Lost your money—and can't get home—and got some kids, too, waiting for you, I dare say?"

"Any amount of 'em," sobbed Toad. "And they'll be hungry—and playing with matches—and upsetting lamps, the little innocents! O dear, O dear!"

"Well, I'll tell you what I'll do," said the good engine-driver. "I'm an engine-driver, as you well may see, and there's no denying it's terribly dirty work. If you'll wash a few shirts for me when you get home, and send 'em along, I'll give you a ride on my engine."

The Toad's misery turned into rapture as he eagerly scrambled up into the cab of the engine. He began to skip up and down and shout and sing snatches of song, to the great astonishment of the engine-driver, who had come across washerwomen before, but never one at all like this. The guard waved his welcome flag and the train moved out of the station.

As they had covered many and many a mile, Toad began considering what he would have for supper, when he noticed that the engine-driver, with a puzzled expression on his face, was leaning over the side of the engine and listening hard. "It's very strange; we're the last train running in this direction tonight, yet I could be sworn that I heard another following us!" Toad became grave and depressed, and a dull pain in the lower part of his spine, communicating itself to his legs, made him want to sit down.

By this time the moon was shining brightly, and the engine-driver, steadying himself on the coal, could command a view of the line behind them for a long distance.

Presently he called out, "I can see it clearly now! It is an engine, on our rails, coming along at a great pace! It looks as if we were being pursued!"

The miserable Toad, crouching in the coal-dust, tried hard to think of something to do, with dismal want of success.

"They are gaining on us fast!" cried the engine-driver. And the engine is crowded with the queerest lot of people! Policemen in their helmets waving and shouting "'Stop, stop, stop!'"

Then Toad fell on his knees among the coals and cried, "Save me, dear kind Mr. Engine-driver, and I will confess everything! I am not the simple washerwoman I seem to be! I am a toad—the well-known and popular Mr. Toad, a landed proprietor; I have just escaped, by my great daring and cleverness, from a loathsome dungeon into which my enemies had flung me; and if those fellows on that engine recapture me, it will be chains and misery once more for poor, unhappy, innocent Toad!"

The engine-driver looked down upon him very sternly, and said, "Now tell the truth, what were you put in prison for?"

"It was nothing very much," said poor Toad, colouring deeply. "I only borrowed a motor-car. I didn't mean to steal it, really; but people—especially magistrates—take such harsh views of thoughtless and high-spirited actions."

The engine-driver looked very grave and said, "I fear that you have been indeed a

wicked toad, and by rights I ought to give you up to offended justice. But you are evidently in sore trouble and distress, so I will not desert you. A short way ahead of us is a long tunnel, and on the other side of that the line passes through a thick wood. Now, I will put on all the speed I can while we are running through the tunnel, but the other fellows will slow down a bit, naturally, for fear of an accident. When we are through, I will shut off steam and put on brakes as hard as I can, and the moment it's safe to do so you must jump and hide in the wood, before they get through the tunnel and see you. Then I will go full speed ahead again, and they can chase me if they like. Now mind and be ready to jump when I tell you!"

They piled on more coals, and the train shot into the tunnel, and the engine rushed and roared and rattled, till at last they shot out at the other side. The driver shut off steam and put on brakes, the Toad got down on the step, and as the train slowed down he heard the driver call out, "Now, jump!"

Toad jumped, rolled down a short embankment, picked himself up unhurt, scrambled into the wood and hid. Out of the tunnel burst the pursuing engine, roaring and whistling, her motley crew waving their various weapons and shouting, "Stop! stop! stop!" When they were past, the Toad had a hearty laugh.

But he soon stopped laughing when he came to consider that it was now very late and dark and cold, and he was in an unknown wood, with no money and no chance of supper. He found the wood strange and unfriendly. Cold, hungry, and tired out, he sought the shelter of a hollow tree and slept soundly till the morning.

Toad was called at an early hour by the exceeding coldness of his toes. Sitting up, he rubbed his eyes first and his complaining toes next, wondered for a moment where he was, then, with a leap of the heart, he remembered everything—his escape, his flight, his pursuit; remembered, first and best thing of all, that he was free!

Free! The word and the thought alone were worth fifty blankets. He was warm from end to end as he thought of the jolly world outside, waiting eagerly for him to make his triumphal entrance. He shook himself and combed the dry leaves out of his hair with his fingers and marched forth into the comfortable morning sun. He had the world all to himself that early summer morning. He sang as he walked, and he walked as he sang, and got more inflated every minute.

After some miles of country lanes, he reached the high road, and as he turned into it and glanced along its white length, he saw approaching him a speck that turned into a dot and then into a blob, and then into something very familiar; and a double note of warning, only too well known, fell on his delighted ear.

"This is something like!" said the excited Toad. "This is real life again, this is once more the great world from which I have been missed so long! I will hail them, my brothers of the wheel, and pitch them a yarn and they will give me a lift, of course, and then I will talk to them some more; and, perhaps, with luck, it may even end in my driving up to Toad Hall in a motor-car! That will be one in the eye for Badger!"

He stepped confidently out into the road when suddenly he became very pale, his heart turned to water, his knees shook and yielded under him, and he doubled up and collapsed. And well he might, the unhappy animal; for the approaching car was the very one he had stolen out of the yard on that fatal day when all his troubles began!

The terrible motor-car drew slowly nearer and nearer, till at last he heard it stop just short of him. Two gentlemen got out and walked round to him and one of them said, "O dear! This is very sad! Here is a poor old thing—a washerwoman apparently—who has fainted in the road! Let us lift her into the car and take her to the nearest village."

They tenderly lifted Toad into the motor-car and propped him up with soft cushions, and proceeded on their way.

"Thank you kindly, Sir," said Toad in a feeble voice. "I'm feeling a great deal better! I was thinking, if I might sit on the front seat there, beside the driver, where I could get the fresh air full in my face, I should soon be all right again."

"Of course you shall," said the gentleman, carefully helping Toad into the front seat. Toad was almost himself again by now. He sat up, looked about him, and tried to beat down the tremors, the yearnings, the old cravings that rose up and beset him and took possession of him entirely.

"It is fate!" he said to himself. "Why strive? Why struggle?" and he turned to the driver at his side.

"Please, Sir," he said, "I wish you would kindly let me try and drive the car for a little. I've been watching you carefully, and I should like to be able to tell my friends that once I had driven a motor-car!"

"Bravo, ma'am! I like your spirit," said the driver. "Let her have a try, and look after her. She won't do any harm."

Toad eagerly scrambled into the seat vacated by the driver, took the steering-wheel in his hands, listened with affected humility to the instructions given him, and set the car in motion, but very slowly and carefully at first, for he was determined to be prudent.

The gentlemen behind clapped their hands and applauded, and Toad heard them saying, "How well she does it! Fancy a washerwoman driving a car as well as that, the first time!"

Toad went a little faster; then faster still, and faster. He heard the gentlemen call out warningly, "Be careful, washerwoman!" And this annoyed him, and he began to lose his head.

"Washerwoman, indeed!" he shouted recklessly. "Ho! ho! I am the Toad, the motor-car snatcher, the prison-breaker, the Toad who always escapes! Sit still, and you shall know what driving really is!"

With a cry of horror, the whole party rose and flung themselves on him. With a half-turn of the wheel, the Toad sent the car crashing through the low hedge. Toad found himself flying through the air with a strong upward rush and then he landed on his back with a thump, in the soft rich grass of a meadow. Sitting up, he could just see the motor-car in the pond, nearly submerged; the gentlemen and the driver, encumbered by their long coats, were floundering helplessly in the water.

He picked himself up rapidly, and set off running across country as hard as he could, scrambling through hedges till he was breathless and weary. When he had recovered his breath somewhat, he laughed till he had to sit down. "Ho, ho!" he cried, "Toad again! Toad, as usual, comes out on the top!"

A slight noise at a distance behind him made him turn his head and look. O horror! O misery! O despair! About two fields off, a chauffeur in his leather gaiters and two large rural policemen were visible, running towards him as hard as they could go!

On he ran desperately, but kept looking back, and saw they still gained steadily. In his blind panic, Toad ran straight into the river! He found himself head over ears in deep water, rapid water that bore him along with a force he could not contend with. Presently he saw that he was approaching a big dark hole in the bank, just above his head, and as the stream bore him past, he reached up with a paw and caught hold of the edge and held on. He drew himself up out of the water, till at last he was able to rest his elbows on the edge of a big dark hole in the bank. As he sighed and blew and stared before him into the dark hole, some bright small thing shone and twinkled in its depths, moving towards him. As it approached, a face grew up gradually around it, and it was a familiar face—the Water Rat!

One, two,
buckle my shoe;

Three, four,
knock at the door;

Five, six,
pick up sticks;

Seven, eight
lay them straight;

Nine, ten,
a good fat hen;

Eleven, twelve,
dig and delve;

Thirteen, fourteen,
maids a-courting;

Fifteen, sixteen
maids in the kitchen;

Seventeen, eighteen,
maids a-waiting;

Nineteen, twenty,
my plate's empty.